NFC SOUTH

BY MICHAEL TEITELBAUM

★ Atlanta Falcons ★ Carolina Panthers ★ New Orleans Saints ★ Tampa Bay Buccaneers ★

Published by The Child's World®
1980 Lookout Drive
Mankato, MN 56003-1705
800-599-READ
www.childsworld.com

The Child's World®: Mary Berendes, Publishing Director
The Design Lab: Kathleen Petelinsek, Design
Editorial Directions, Inc.: Pam Mamsch and E. Russell Primm,
Project Managers

Photographs ©: Robbins Photography

Library of Congress Cataloging-in-Publication Data
Teitelbaum, Michael.
  NFC South / by Michael Teitelbaum.
    p. cm. Includes bibliographical references and index.
  ISBN 978-1-60973-133-5 (library reinforced : alk. paper)
  1. National Football Conference—Juvenile literature.
2. Football—Southern States—Juvenile literature. I. Title.
  GV950.7.T44 2011
  796.332'640973—dc22   2011007153

Printed in the United States of America
Mankato, MN
April 2012
PA02132

TABLE OF
CONTENTS

NFC
SOUTH

4

First Season: 1966
NFL Championships: 0
Colors: Red, Black,
Silver, and White
Mascot: Freddie Falcon

ATLANTA
FALCONS

BIRDS OF PREY

The Atlanta Falcons joined the NFL as an **expansion team** in 1966. They got off to a rough start. They didn't have their first winning season until 1971. In 1980 they played to an impressive 12–4 record. The Falcons were eliminated in the playoffs that year by Dallas, who staged an amazing fourth-quarter comeback.

The Falcons have never won an NFL championship. They had their best season in 1998, going 14–2. That year they made it to the Super Bowl—the only time they have made it to the big game—but lost to the Denver Broncos 34–19.

Matt Ryan was the first rookie quarterback in the Falcons' history to lead the team to an 11-win season.

HOME FIELD

The Falcons play in the Georgia Dome, which has been their home since 1992. The Dome is the world's largest cable-supported stadium. It also hosted several events during the Olympics in 1996!

BIG DAYS

* In 1978, the Falcons made the playoffs for the first time. They beat the Philadelphia Eagles in the first round but lost to the Dallas Cowboys in the second round.
* In 1998, the Falcons made it to the Super Bowl for the first time. They lost to the Denver Broncos 34–19.
* The Falcons returned to the NFC Championship Game in 2004, but lost to the Eagles 27–10 and didn't make it to the Super Bowl.

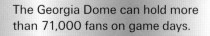

The Georgia Dome can hold more than 71,000 fans on game days.

SUPERSTARS!

★

THEN

Steve Bartkowski, quarterback: field general for the team from 1975 to 1985

Claude Humphrey, defensive end: core member of the defense in the 1960s and '70s

Tommy Nobis, linebacker: defensive standout from 1966 to 1976

★

NOW

Matt Ryan, quarterback: completes more than 62 percent of his passes

Michael Turner, running back: the team's leading rusher

Roddy White, wide receiver: speedy player who averages almost eight catches per game

★

STAT LEADERS

(All-time team leaders*)

Passing Yards: Steve Bartkowski, 23,470

Rushing Yards: Gerald Riggs, 6,631

Receiving Yards: Terance Mathis, 7,349

Touchdowns: Terance Mathis, 57

Interceptions: Rolland Lawrence, 39

★

(*Through 2010 season.)

TIMELINE

1966
NFL expansion gives birth to Atlanta Falcons.

1971
Falcons experience their first winning season and their first trip to the postseason.

1980
Falcons win their division for the first time.

Wide receiver Roddy White made Pro Bowl appearances in 2008 and 2009.

1997
Falcons make their first Super Bowl appearance, losing to the Broncos.

2004
Falcons return to the NFC Championship Game, but lose to the Eagles.

First Season: 1995
NFL Championships: 0
Colors: Black, Blue, and
      Silver
Mascot: Sir Purr

CAROLINA
PANTHERS

BIG CATS

The Carolina Panthers came into the NFL in 1995 as an expansion team, along with the Jacksonville Jaguars. That year the Panthers posted the best record ever for an NFL expansion team, going 7–9. Then, in only their second season, the Panthers finished 12–4, making it all the way to the NFC Championship Game.

Following the 2003 season, the Panthers reached the Super Bowl. They lost to the New England Patriots in one of the most exciting Super Bowls in history. With only seconds left and the game tied, New England kicked a game-winning field goal to beat the Panthers.

Charles Godfrey was the first Panthers safety to start all 16 games of his rookie season.

HOME FIELD

The Panthers play in Bank of America Stadium, which was known as Ericsson Stadium until 2003. More than 73,000 Panthers fans can enjoy the action here at every game.

BIG DAYS

* In only their second season in the league, the Carolina Panthers made it to the playoffs.
* In one of the most exciting Super Bowls ever, held in 2004, the Panthers staged a late comeback to tie the New England Patriots 29–29. The Panthers lost on a last-second field goal 32–29.
* The Panthers made it back to the NFC Championship Game in 2005 but lost to the Seattle Seahawks 34–14.

Bank of America Stadium is located in Charlotte, North Carolina.

SUPERSTARS!

★

THEN

Kerry Collins, quarterback: offensive leader for the team's first three seasons

Willie Green, wide receiver: top receiver in the team's early years

Reggie White, defensive end: first Panther to be in the Hall of Fame

★

NOW

Charles Godfrey, safety: strong defensive player

Matt Moore, quarterback: current team leader, completing more than 50 percent of his passes

Steve Smith, wide receiver: Panthers' all-time best player

DeAngelo Williams, running back: top rusher on the team

★

STAT LEADERS

(All-time team leaders*)

Passing Yards: Jake Delhomme, 19,258

Rushing Yards: DeAngelo Williams, 4,211

Receiving Yards: Muhsin Muhammad, 9,255

Touchdowns: Steve Smith, 60

Interceptions: Eric Davis, 25

★

(*Through 2010 season.)

TIMELINE

1995	1996	2003
Carolina Panthers enter the league.	Panthers make the playoffs in just their second season.	Panthers make it to the Super Bowl but lose to New England.

Running back DeAngelo Williams was selected to his first Pro Bowl in 2009.

2005

Panthers return to the NFC Championship Game but fail to advance to the Super Bowl.

2008

Panthers post a 12–4 record and earn a trip to the playoffs.

First Season: 1967
NFL Championships: 1
Colors: Black and Gold
Mascots: Gumbo and
Sir Saint

NEW ORLEANS
SAINTS

WHO DAT?

The New Orleans Saints entered the NFL as an expansion team for the 1967 season. It would be 20 years before they had a .500 season, and 20 years until they finally put together a winning season.

From 1987 to 1992, the Saints made the playoffs four times. They finally won a playoff game in 2000, defeating the **defending** Super Bowl champs, the St. Louis Rams. They reached the NFC Championship Game in 2006 but lost to the Bears. Then, in an inspirational victory, the Saints won the Super Bowl after the 2009 season. The team lifted the spirits of a city still **devastated** by Hurricane Katrina, which had struck in 2005.

Quarterback Drew Brees played five seasons for the San Diego Chargers before joining the Saints for the 2006 season.

HOME FIELD

The Saints play in the Louisiana Superdome. The Superdome was used as a place for people to ride out Hurricane Katrina in 2005. But the roof gave in, and the scene inside became desperate. The Saints played their home games elsewhere in 2005, then returned home to the Superdome following a $185 million **renovation** of the stadium.

BIG DAYS

* In 2000, after being in the NFL for 33 years, the Saints finally won their first playoff game.
* As the 2005 NFL season was about to begin, Hurricane Katrina struck New Orleans, destroying a huge portion of the city.
* In 2009, with America rooting for them, the Saints brought a smile to their devastated city by beating the heavily favored Indianapolis Colts 31–17 in the Super Bowl. The league's **laughingstock** was finally a champion.

The Louisiana Superdome opened in 1975.

SUPERSTARS!

★

THEN

Earl Campbell, running back: Hall of Famer who played
two seasons with the Saints

Rickey Jackson, linebacker: 12-season tough defensive player

Archie Manning, quarterback: the father of two current NFL
quarterbacks was an early fan favorite

Jim Taylor, running back: this Hall of Famer finished his career with
the Saints

★

NOW

Drew Brees, quarterback: led the Saints to their Super Bowl victory

Reggie Bush, running back: top offensive weapon

Marques Colston, wide receiver: the team's top receiver

Jonathan Vilma, linebacker: one of the top defensive players in the league

★

STAT LEADERS

(All-time team leaders*)

Passing Yards: Drew Brees, 22,918

Rushing Yards: Deuce McAllister, 6,096

Receiving Yards: Eric Martin, 7,854

Touchdowns: Deuce McAllister, 55

Interceptions: Dave Waymer, 37

★

(*Through 2010 season.)

TIMELINE

1967	1979	1987	1990–1992
New Orleans Saints join the NFL.	Saints have their first .500 season.	Saints have their first winning season, going 12–4 and making the playoffs for the first time.	Saints make the playoffs three seasons in a row.

Running back Reggie Bush was the second overall pick in the 2006 NFL Draft.

2000
Saints win their first division championship.

2005
New Orleans is devastated by Hurricane Katrina.

2009
Saints win the Super Bowl, beating the Indianapolis Colts.

First Season: 1976
NFL Championships: 1
Colors: Red, Pewter,
Orange, and Black
Mascot: Captain Fear
the Buccaneer

TAMPA BAY
BUCCANEERS

AHOY, MATES!

When the Tampa Bay Buccaneers, or "Bucs" as their fans call them, joined the NFL in 1976, they were in the AFC. The Bucs went 0–14 their first season. The following year, they switched over to the NFC.

In 1979 they had their first winning record and also made the playoffs for the first time. They went all the way to the NFC Championship Game. There they lost to the Los Angeles Rams 9–0. The Bucs returned to the NFC Championship Game in 1999 and 2002. In 2002 they beat the Eagles. They then went on to win the Super Bowl, defeating the Oakland Raiders 48–21.

Quarterback Josh Freeman holds the Bucs team records for rookie season passing yards and rookie season touchdown passes.

HOME FIELD

The Bucs have played their home games in Raymond James Stadium since 1998. A copy of an 1800s pirate ship is permanently harbored in Buccaneer Cove. Loud cannons fire seven times when the Bucs score a touchdown!

BIG DAYS

* In 1979, in only their fourth year in the league, the Bucs went all the way to the NFC Championship Game.
* In 1999, the Bucs returned to the NFL Championship Game, where they almost came from behind. But a **replay** ruled that Bert Emmanuel did not make a catch that it appeared he had made.
* In 2003, the Bucs won their first Super Bowl. After beating San Francisco and Philadelphia in the playoffs, they crushed the Oakland Raiders 48–21 in the big game.

Raymond James Stadium seats up to 65,890 fans.

SUPERSTARS!

★

THEN

Randall McDaniel, guard: Hall of Fame lineman who played the final
two years of his 14-year career with the Bucs
Lee Roy Selmon, defensive end: Hall of Famer who anchored the
Bucs' defense for nine seasons
Steve Young, quarterback: Hall of Famer who began his
13-year NFL career with the Bucs

★

NOW

LeGarrette Blount, running back: team's leading rusher
Josh Freeman, quarterback: starter completes more than
60 percent of his passes
Aqib Talib, cornerback: leads the team in interceptions
Mike Williams, wide receiver: Bucs' top receiver

★

STAT LEADERS
(All-time team leaders*)
Passing Yards: Vinny Testaverde, 14,820
Rushing Yards: James Wilder, 5,957
Receiving Yards: Mark Carrier, 5,018
Touchdowns: Mike Alstott, 71
Interceptions: Ronde Barber, 40

★

(*Through 2010 season.)

TIMELINE

1976
Tampa Bay Buccaneers enter the NFL in the AFC.

1977
Bucs switch to the NFC.

1979
Bucs make the playoffs for the first time.

Cornerback Aqib Talib was the only the second Bucs player in history to record three interceptions in a single game.

1999–2002
Bucs make the playoffs four seasons in a row.

2002
Bucs win their first Super Bowl.

STAT
STUFF

★

NFC SOUTH DIVISION STATISTICS*

Team	All-Time Record (W-L-T)	NFL Titles (Most Recent)	Times in NFL Playoffs
Atlanta Falcons	289–393–6	0	10
Carolina Panthers	119–137–0	0	4
New Orleans Saints	286–383–5	1 (2009)	7
Tampa Bay Buccaneers	218–329–1	1 (2002)	10

★

NFC SOUTH DIVISION CHAMPIONSHIPS
(MOST RECENT)

Atlanta Falcons . . . 4 (2010)

Carolina Panthers . . . 3 (2008)

New Orleans Saints . . . 4 (2009)

Tampa Bay Buccaneers . . . 6 (2007)

★

(*Through 2010 season.)

NFC SOUTH PRO FOOTBALL
HALL OF FAME MEMBERS

Atlanta Falcons

Deion Sanders, CB

New Orleans Saints

Doug Atkins, DE

Jim Finks, General manager

Rickey Jackson, LB

Tampa Bay Buccaneers

Lee Roy Selmon, DE

NOTE: Includes players with at least three seasons with the team. Players may appear with more than one team.

Position Key:
QB: Quarterback
RB: Running back
WR: Wide receiver
G: Guard
LB: Linebacker
DE: Defensive end

GLOSSARY

★

anchored (ANG-kurd): to keep something in place, for example, by being a leader

defending (di-FEND-ngh): current title holder

devastated (DEV-uh-stayt-uhd): destroyed

expansion team (ek-SPAN-shuhn TEEM): a club added to a league that makes the league bigger

laughingstock (LAFF-ingh-stahk): something that is always made fun of

renovation (ren-uh-VAY-shuhn): rebuilding an existing structure

replay (REE-play): looking at a recording of a play to see if officials made the correct call

FIND OUT MORE

★

BOOKS

Buckley, James, Jr. *Scholastic Ultimate Guide to Football.*
New York: Franklin Watts, 2009.

MacRae, Sloan. *The New Orleans Saints.* New York:
PowerKids Press, 2011.

Stewart, Mark. *The Atlanta Falcons.* Chicago:
Norwood House Press, 2009.

Stewart, Mark. *The Carolina Panthers.*
Chicago: Norwood House Press, 2008.

Stewart, Mark. *The Tampa Bay Buccaneers.* Chicago:
Norwood House Press, 2009.

★

WEB SITES

For links to learn more about football visit
www.childsworld.com/links

Note to Parents, Teachers, and Librarians: We routinely verify our Web links to make sure
they are safe and active sites. So encourage your readers to check them out!

INDEX

ABOUT THE AUTHOR

Michael Teitelbaum has been a writer and editor of children's books and magazines for more than twenty years. He was editor of *Little League Magazine* and *Spider-Man Magazine* for Marvel Comics. He is the author of a two-volume encyclopedia on the Baseball Hall of Fame. Teitelbaum and his wife, Sheleigh, live in a 170-year-old farmhouse in the Catskill Mountains of upstate New York.